Ernest Whitney

Legends of the Pike's Peak region

The sacred myths of the Manitcu

Ernest Whitney

Legends of the Pike's Peak region
The sacred myths of the Manitou

ISBN/EAN: 9783337151867

Printed in Europe, USA, Canada, Australia, Japan

Cover: Foto ©Andreas Hilbeck / pixelio.de

More available books at **www.hansebooks.com**

LEGENDS

OF THE

PIKE'S PEAK REGION

The Sacred Myths of the Manitou

BY

ERNEST WHITNEY, M. A.

ASSISTED BY

WILLIAM S. ALEXANDER

ILLUSTRATED BY THOMAS C. PARRISH

PUBLISHED BY

THE CHAIN & HARDY CO
DENVER, COLORADO
1892

ILLUSTRATIONS.

OWEVER un-
couth they may be,
the myths and le-
gends of early na-
tions, like the po-
etry of later, give
the highest and
truest exponents of their characters, and preserve with a singular fidelity the very essence
of their daily lives, their fears and hopes, their
assumptions and intuitions. It is proverbial

that the songs of a people are stronger than their laws; and the myths and traditions embodying the sentiments upon which national character, national religion, are founded, are more powerful than the songs, which they inspire. A ballad of the people, a bit of folk lore, may teach us more than whole chapters of history; we can hardly understand history without such lights.

A century ago Scotland was to England what Bœotia was to cultured Athens, proverbially the land of the uninteresting, the kingdom of dullness and prose; yet every lake and stream, every glen and rock wore the halo of poetry, the glamour of romance; and when the Wizard of the North drew aside the veil of prejudice, the eyes of all England were opened as to visions, and the "land of the mountain and the flood" became as familiar and dear as the favored haunts of home. Scott had discovered a new world, new even to the dwellers in it. Gathering the tangled, distorted fragments of tradition floating about his native hills and dales, traditions full of romance, yet despised or belittled as trifles even by those from whom he learned them, he gave to the world such pleasures of entertainment as it had seldom known before. And he gave to his country fame, and the intellectual stimulus which led to its prosperity. Thenceforth Scotland was one of the beloved spots of the earth. Our historian, Prescott, states that after the publication of "'The Lady of the Lake' the post-horse duty rose to an extraordinary degree in Scotland from the eagerness of travelers to visit the localities of the poem." Another has said that indeed the race of tourists was called into existence by the pen of Scott.

What those neglected legends were to Scotland, Colorado's are to her. We scan the glories of her scenery, surpassing the marvels of the Alps, the beauties of the Rhine, and lament the absence of tradition to give them the charm of Old World scenes. The tourist notes this seeming sterility with a touch of prejudice. "But where are your traditions?" is the final question; and the answer is, "We have none; our history is too recent." Yet the romantic Rhine cliffs, or even the land of sphinx and pyramid, did nc . rise above the ocean until its waves had beaten for ages at the base of Rocky Mountain peaks. This is the Old World, Europe and India are of the New.   And if nature in fantastic play has made this the world's wonderland, much more has man through centuries written and rewritten its fading pages with the mysteries of immemorial myths, legends, and traditions. From Pike's Peak to Popocatepetl the land is a palimpsest, dotted with ruins of remotest antiquity, the relics of a people whose records are replete with poetry and strange romance. Their manuscripts enrich the archives of Mexico and Madrid, and yet we learn but little of them.   They moulder in the missions of the suspicious Spanish priests, or among the mystic treasures of the Pueblos, and are decaying unread.   When we come northward to the paths of later pioneers, to lands of less civilized races, where history lives by oral transmission only, hardly a legend but has lapsed into oblivion.   Those only can live which are united to something concrete and enduring, or which are so vitally interwoven that the life of one tradition insures the life of another.   The early hunters looked upon natives whom they met as savage aliens rather than possibly kindred beings, and cared more for their furs and gold dust than for any history of their peoples.   But even yet much may be regained from a study of the records of Spanish priests, from the lips of living races, and from the thickly scattered ruins, many of which are even yet undiscovered, nearly all of which are practically uninvestigated.   Indeed, much has been regained, and from the mass of material in the collections of Bancroft and others, and from results of original research, the present writer has sought to extract what is most interesting to the audience to whom this little book is offered.

The perhaps most remarkable cycle of myths north of Mexico, the Sacred Myths of the Manitou, might have perished, or lost their home and identity at least, in another decade, though the loss of such interesting relics of aboriginal thought would have seemed inexcusable.   But what we yet retain is sufficient to appeal to the imagination most vividly, and its restoration in this late day seems almost to partake of the nature of strange revelation. We ask who were the people among whom such fables originated. The question as to the identity of the earliest inhabitants in the Pike's Peak region is a difficult one to answer, but the conclusion of the latest historian is that a race which had made considerable progress in civilization dwelt for centuries in Colorado. Then a more barbarous people encroached upon its territory, and it was crowded southward step by step, advancing in civilization as it was driven from barbarism, leaving picturesque ruins along its later path. It is the conjecture of many students that this people was none other than "that mystic race of Aztlan, who, ages before, had descended into the valley [of Mexico] like an inundation from the north; the race whose religion was founded upon credulity; the race full of chivalry, but horribly governed by a crafty priesthood."

The situation of Aztlan, the ancient home of the Aztecs, is the most puzzling question in Mexican history. At all events, it was almost

certainly north of Mexico, but whether it
linked the home of the Aztec and Toltec to
California on the northwest, or to Colorado on
the northeast, it seems impossible for the un-
prejudiced historian to decide.   The latest
and safest guide through the conflict of varying assertions, Mr. Justin Winsor, represents a
consensus of the wisest and most conservative
opinions.   He is inclined to believe that un-
doubtedly two streams of immigration, one on
each side of the Rocky Mountains, flowed
together into Mexico. Toltec tradition tells
of a long sojourn some twelve centuries ago in
a land called Hue Hue Tlapallan, which means
"Old Red Land," and a local historian has
called attention to its hint of Colorado—

"Which fair Columbia, bending toward the West,
Now wears a crimson rose upon her breast—"

land of "crimson-hued rocks and yellow
plains," the "land of red earth."   Certainly no
place but the wonderful Grand Caverns of
Manitou and the several caves of William's
Canon has been found in the probable range
of Aztec migration, which can be so well ident-

ified with the mysterious "Seven Caves" of
Aztlan, so often mentioned in Mexican myths.
It was the sacred birth-place of their great
god Huitzil, and to it sacerdotal embassies
were sent even as late as the year before the
invasion of Cortez.   The early explorer whose
name the great mountain now bears, shows
that a Via Sacra from Mexico northward to
the peak was long kept open.   "Indeed," Pike
wrote of the mountain in 1806, "it was so remarkable as to be known by all the savage
nations for hundreds of miles around, and to
be spoken of with admiration by the Spaniards
of New Mexico, and was the bound of their
travels northwest."   It is not unlikely that the
knowledge of an open and traveled path, and
the belief that it led to temples rich in gold
and jewels, led the earlier Spaniards to their
northern settlements   and   later   excursions.
The tribe of Montezuma was but one of a
group of tribes each of which contributed its
quota to the phenomenal civilization of the
empire of Anahuac during the fifteenth and six-
teenth centuries.   Even granting that neither
Aztecs nor Toltecs rose in Colorado, it may

still be confidently believed that at least one of
the most important Nahuan nations learned its
early lessons of barbaric culture under the
tuition of Pike's Peak. And this tribe or nation during the slow migration, or soon after,
was completely absorbed by the Aztec stream,
if it was not the leader of it. What more
probable? If it did not join this stream what
was its fate?

THEN in these "Sacred Myths of the Manitou," we perhaps see reflected some dim germs of that wonderful religion, which was at once the strength and weakness of the illustrious victims of Cortez.

Five, ten, or perhaps fifteen centuries ago the dwellers along the great mountain slope and adjacent plains had learned to look upon that region around the eastern base of Pike's Peak as one made sacred by a thousand

powerful associations. The great peak seen forty leagues away, towering among and wedged between the stars, "pinnacled dim in the intense inane," was to them the symbol of a god, the abode of the All-Father, the wigwam of the Manitou. The wide ranges of alps on either side of it—the broad plains sublime in their infinity—even the mysteriously-born Father of Waters—none of these had the influence upon the superstitious and superreligious native which was exerted by that ever-watching warden of the west. Probably these early comers first saw the mountain after months of dreary wanderings over the desolate prairies. Awful in loneliness when seen afar, silent and motionless as death, they drew near and found it filled with life strange and ennobling, and with a kindly nature, ready to stoop and mingle with the human and make them rich with blessings. It was a mountain of mystery. To the dwellers on the monotonous eastern levels, its ever varying miracles of light and shadow were revelations of infinite spiritual power, and the sun-worshiper was ever drawn nearer to its presence where the mysterious manifestations could be better seen. If the hunter wandered out of its sight, it was at times perhaps with a feeling of relief, as at escaping from an almost burdensome oversight; yet he dared not stay long in the lands lying beyond its guardianship. It was a never forgotten element in life. If he slew the deer or buffalo, a quick word of gratitude was sent across the plains. If sometime a dark thought came to him, he glanced furtively at this reader of thoughts, and faltered. If in lone venturing, perils confronted him, he would lift up his eyes to the hills whence came his help, and go forward with new courage. If the tribes rallied for the war path, they sat in reverence and hope before this god of peaceful heavens, until tempest darkened and hid his face, and then like storm swept down to certain victory. But if this oracle gave no show of anger, rash was the chieftain who dare attack a foe save in absolute and immediate self-defense.

The story is told that a great and powerful nation from remote regions once invaded the lands of the children of the Manitou.

Day after day the war band advanced toward this heart of the empire, and every day the threateningly severe mountain-god seemed more remote, more terrible, than before, until at last, overcome with superstitious dread, they turned back, believing it was impossible to harm his people or do battle in his awful presence.

Such were some of the thoughts which this mysterious mountain inspired in primitive minds. To them whatever of nature was strange, beautiful, sublime, or powerful, was worshipful. It was not unnatural that the mountain should become dominant in their religious system. Sun worshipers already, what sublimer, nobler idolatry could there be than theirs for this priest of the sun in the land of undimmed heavens! Even the pilgrim of to-day would fain uncover and bend the knee before its tonsured head. That colossal Face upon the mountain side was the first of all American idols.

Civilization made progress among the chosen people here, and there was much of nobility and thoughtfulness in individual characters. Their climate, the gift of the Manitou, made them a strong race physically, but they were, perhaps, chiefly feared and respected for their institutions and their distinguished religion. We have records full of detail of religious systems far more remarkable, or more completely developed, among the Nahuan nations. Torquemada estimates the number of temples in Anahuac to have been 80,000, and Clavigero places the number of priests in these temples at 1,000,000. Every year twenty to fifty-thousand human beings were sacrificed on their altars. The myths and fables of their religion fill huge volumes. But probably nowhere north of Old Mexico can be found traces of a theology anywhere nearly approaching in simplicity and granduer this one which had its Ararat, its Eden, and its Salem in the Pike's Peak region. For here they looked as to the cradle and the Mecca of their race. The scant reflections which are given of this religion to-day, like the clouds of a fading sunset, can barely suggest the glory of that sunset, the wide-streaming radiance of the by-gone day.

The archæologist, tracing the religious history of the Greeks, finds in the early home of one of their tribes the ruins of a temple, and the torsos and other fragments of a group of statues.   It is his first duty to preserve these exactly as they are found.   It is a second obligation so to study the temple, and the arrangement of the sculptured fragments around and within it, that, if possible, he may understand and interpret the spiritual meaning of the whole, as an exponent of the religion.   In this work he will take assistance from history and from myth, and he will be aided by comparison with other temples.   If obvious portions of the original group are hopelessly missing, his special knowledge may warrant the restoration of an arm or head or possibly an entire figure.   After the manner of the archæologist, we have delved among the ruins of a forsaken temple.   We have studied the history, actual and mythical, of the race who revered its shrines.   And with the best lights vouchsafed to us, we have tried to give, in a form agreeable to the general reader, our restoration of the myths of that ancient religion. If we have felt it necessary here and there to add a touch of completeness almost arbitrarily, we have been so guided by careful study of the myth makers and of cognate religions as to feel warranted in each case.

The breath and finer spirit of a purely human religion, if any religion is purely human, is not always well shown in those myths and fables which are its most conspicuous chronicles for later times. The fables may be full of the grotesque and the absurd, mere blind and awkward gropings after a system where all was vague and mystic at first. The first explanation of a crude theolgy will, it is likely, be accepted as the best. And in process of oral transmission through generations all the myths will suffer strange modifications without losing their main identity. Thus none of the earliest names of the deities in the myths before us have been preserved, and Manitou, the common name of the supreme deity of the later races, has been adopted from the legends of later tribes.

The origin of a cycle of myths like the one we are interested in was probably very much in this wise, if we may trust the teaching of analogy. A tribe, naturally of a roving disposition, driven from their river home by a series of devastating floods, strikes boldly out for new fortunes in the unknown prairies. Long, toilsome journeys bring them at last to the foot of the peak, where they make a new home, won by the genial climate, fertile soil, and varied topography. Gradually the tribe increases, its power spreads, and it controls all the region round about. It is called the Mountain Tribe. Its members are children of the Mountain. It is not long before these dwellers by the Wigwam of the Manitou are called children of the Manitou, and they believe in a god as their creator and the mountain as their birthplace. Later the story develops into the true mythological form, uniting their earlier and later religious ideas; and traditions common to all races of mankind, wherever found, are woven into it. So in its later shape we have the following:

At the beginning of all things the Lesser

Spirits possessed the earth, and dwelt near the banks of the Great River. They had created a race of men to be their servants, but these men were far inferior to the present inhabitants of the earth, and made endless trouble for their creators. Therefore the Lesser Spirits resolved to destroy mankind and the earth itself; so they caused the Great River to rise until it burst its banks and overwhelmed everything. They themselves took each a large portion of the best of the earth, that they might create a new world, and a quantity of maize which had been their particular food, and returned to heaven. Arriving at the gate of heaven, which is at the end of the plains, where the sky and the mountains meet, they were told that they could not bring such burdens of earth into heaven. Accordingly they dropped them all then and there. These falling masses made a great heap on the top of the world which rose far above the waters, and this was the origin of Pike's Peak, which is thus shown to be directly under the gate of heaven. Formerly it was twice as high as it is now, but lost its summit as we shall see later on.   The rock masses upon it and all about it, show plainly that they have been dropped from the sky.   The extent and variety of mineral wealth in the region prove that the earth's choicest materials are deposited here.   And still as the constellations move across the heavens and vanish above the mountain summits, we may see the spirits rise from the Great River, and pass to the gate of heaven.   The falling stars are their falling burdens, or the dropping grains of maize.

As the Lesser Spirits held their flight to the gate of heaven from time to time grains of their maize fell to the earth.   These germs being especially blest by their contact with the immortals, sprang up with wonderful vigor even under the waters of the flood, and soon reached the surface, where they quickly ripened.   Now among the inhabitants of the earth left to destruction, was one man who by secretly feeding upon the food of the Spirits, the sacred maize, had become much stronger and superior in every way to his fellow beings. Such was his strength that he succeeded in sustaining himself and his wife above the waters for a very long time. Suddenly a maize stalk rose before him and blossomed into fruit. Breaking a joint from it, he soon fashioned this into a rude boat in which he took refuge with his wife. In commemoration of this the maize stalk was ever after hollowed on one side. Not knowing what direction to take on the pathless waters, he paddled toward the only other object visible upon the face of the deep. On approaching, this proved to be another maize stalk. Upon it were a pair of field mice which shared with him their supply of grain. Launching forth again he paddled toward another object visible in the distance, which proved to be another maize plant. It was held by a pair of gophers which were as generous as the field mice with their corn, and gave enough to sustain life until he reached the next maize plant. Thus unconsciously following the course of the Lesser Spirits, he passed in turn the maize plants of the prairie dog, the squirrel, the rabbit, and all the animals, and then came to the maize plants of the birds, until passing from one to another he came to the mountain. Having landed his

boat upon it, the man died of exhaustion, and ·
the woman died soon after, in the pains of
maternity, giving birth to a boy and girl.

The Spirits, looking down from the gate of
heaven, had watched the long voyage of hard-
ship with deep interest, and their sympathies
were aroused for the forsaken creatures on the
bleak island peak.   Thinking that there was
after all something worth preserving here, they
endowed the infants with gifts raising them
above their ancestors in intelligence and
power.   And feeding upon the sacred maize
which the Spirits had dropped on the top of
the mountain, the children rapidly advanced
to the age of maturity.   One is minded of—

"There shall be a handful of corn in the
earth upon the top of the mountains; the fruit
thereof shall shake like Lebanon; and they of
the city shall flourish like grass of the earth."

Then the Spirits loosed one of the monsters
of heaven, the Lizard Dragon, Thirst.   Seeing
the great satisfaction offered him, the huge
creature plunged directly to the watery world
beneath.   The waters entirely engulfed him,
and for the first time his unquenchable passion

knew something like gratification. He drank and drank and drank, and every day the sea grew lower and the mountain higher, until at last the dragon's body was uncovered. He pursued the waters, still drinking, until they had receded beyond sight. Then fearing he would dry up all the oceans and rivers beyond, the all-powerful Spirits called him back. Seeking to return to the gate of heaven, his wings were unable to carry his swollen body, and he fell back to the earth with such force that his neck was broken off completely, and he lay a huge crushed carcass on the land. Such was the origin of the Mountain of the Dragon, or Cheyenne Mountain as it is called to-day. From his opened neck there issued a torrent of blood and water which made the soil over which it flowed the most fertile in the world. And after all the blood had flowed from his veins, there still issued a stream of the purest water, and the sweetest for quenching the thirst ever known. This fable of the Lizard Dragon, Thirst, is strikingly characteristic of a land where thirst was one of the familiar terrors; and perhaps no creature of

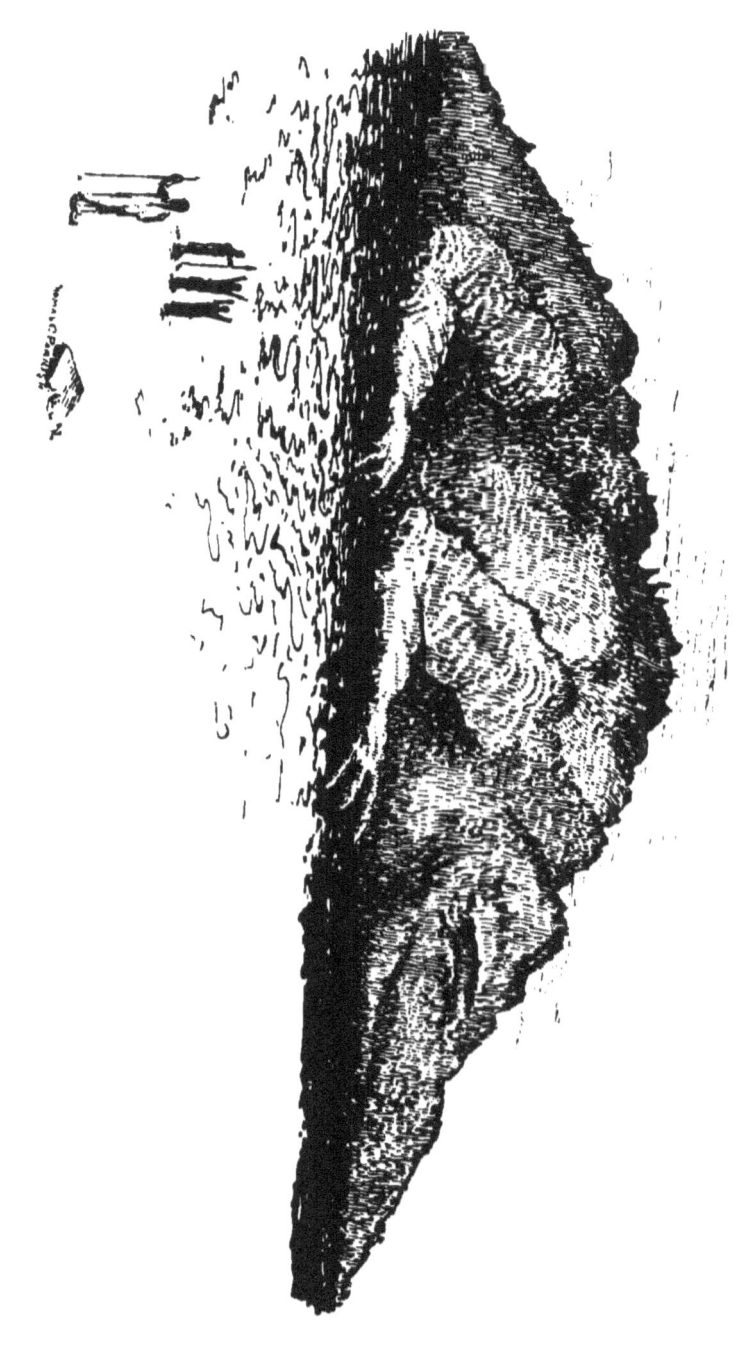

the region is a fitter embodiment of the conception than the lizard, which frequents the dryest places.   There is probably an allusion to this legend in the quaint old Indian chant, which in translation would run as follows:

> "On deer path or war path
> I wish I were like the lizard,
> Never thirsting because his grandfather
> Once had all he wanted to drink.
> But my grandfather was always thirsty."

No one who looks upon Cheyenne from the heights to the east or northeast of the city of Colorado Springs can fail to recognize the bloated form of the petrified monster, even to the spurs upon its back.

The mountain on which the parents of the new race were left was so steep and inaccessible that they could contrive no way to escape from it.   At last when their supply of maize was nearly gone, and the land below began to grow beautiful with new verdure, the Spirits told them to get into the boat and, after the manner of Quetzalcoatl, to slide down.   The track made by the boat may even yet be seen on the eastern face of the mountain, and was a favorite resort of Quetzalcoatl, the sliding god; and the boat itself, the cradle of the race, was of course preserved. From the campus of the college it can best be seen, riding the ridges of the granite waves that flow tumultuously by that eminence west of Cheyenne known as St. Peter's Dome. It is shaped like the familiar birch-bark canoe, curving high at either end, and in it sit two worshipful figures, one plying the paddle. One of the most frequent embellishments in Aztec MSS. pictures such a canoe moving over a flood toward a lone mountain.

At the foot of the mountain they found the most beautiful climate in the world, for being directly under the portals of heaven it shared with the Spirits the overflowing effulgence of celestial light and atmosphere. But the subsiding waters had left about the foot of the mountain all manner of dead creatures, and these with the body of the dragon filled the air with pestilence. Then the parents of mankind prayed to the Spirits for help. And the Spirits heard their prayer. They turned the huge body of the dragon to stone, and they granted to the parents of mankind that this their home should never know the curse of disease, but that it should be held sacred as a place of healing for all the tribes. As a pledge of their promise they sent to them Waters of Life, so that the land was made sweet, the pestilence stayed, and all diseases healed. And such was the origin of the celebrated springs of Manitou, which retain all their miraculous virtues to this day.

For a long time the inhabitants of the earth dwelt in the ease and luxury of a golden age. But soon their numbers so increased that it was no longer easy to live without care, and the people were obliged to diffuse themselves over the region round about. Then came three of the Lesser Spirits, and dwelt among them. One taught them agriculture; from the second they learned how to make weapons and set traps, and hunt successfully; and the third instructed them in religion and government. Each of these Spirits built for himself a magnificent titanic temple and home. Although it is impossible to identify each temple with its particular deity, the three are

are well known by their modern names as The
Garden of the Gods, Glen Eyrie, and Blair
Athol. It was the mission of the third Spirit
to lead them to the worship of the one and
single All Father, the great Manitou, whose
home was in the heaven of heavens, and whose
manifestation was the sun. It is a familiar
fact that the worship of the sun, as the most
obvious type of regenerative life, was one of
the very earliest and most widely spread
germs of religion, not only among the primitive nations of America, but in the Old World
as well. And the purist of to-day who sees
nothing worshipful in these manifestations of
the deity, may by his own misconceptions
know less of some of the attributes of that
deity than did his more reverent fellow in days
of ignorant barbarism.

At first under the instruction of the Spirit,
the people became so enthusiastically faithful
in their devotion to the new religion, that
when their eyes were closed, and even at night
the image of the Manitou ever stood before
them, and tradition tells us that they were
often afflicted with blindness. It was not

unnatural that awe and fear predominated over love in such religion, and that their god was at times a Moloch in their sight. Moreover only the clearer eyes of the royal family and of the higher priestly class, could discern the exact features of the Manitou in that blaze of glory.

At last certain of the people, urged by some of the royal princes, implored the Spirit to intercede for them, and ask the Manitou graciously to throw aside this impenetrable and awful veil of splendor, wherewith he was wont to envelope his countenance, and favor them with a more endurable manifestation of his watchful care. After much persuasion the Spirit consented to undertake the precarious mission.

Soon the people noted that the sun, which had hitherto passed directly above the mountain, was gradually withdrawing towards the south. His warmth lessened, plants perished, and the first Winter came with its new and strange hardships. Flocks of birds were seen flying after the departing sun. Many among the people followed their god, and despondency fell upon the children of the peak when they realized that their Manitou was offended.

But soon those who remained were cheered by a new presence in the heavens, a milder, more acceptable manifestation of the Manitou. The silver moon appeared with its varying phases, now in one part of the sky, now in another, but ever showing clearly to all eyes the plain features of the Manitou. But the Manitou still showed the supremacy of the sun by paling the new image in its presence, and causing the moon to do reverence to the sun by wholly yielding to its glory for some days every month, after which the moon came forth with renewed beauty; for that invisible image in the sun was stamped anew upon the face of the moon each time that it drew near the god of day, thus insuring an accurate reproduction, much to the satisfaction of the thoughtful. These wonderful changes in heaven and earth caused consternation through all neighboring nations, and couriers were sent from tribe to tribe. When it was found that only the children of the peak could explain the inexplicable phenomena, great was the increase of their power and authority.

The reverence for the Manitou now deepened among the people. They found that the rigors of Winter were after all a blessing with few disadvantages. And soon the Manitou became so pleased with the worshipers that he even brought back the sun from the low skies of the south, the birds returned, and some of those who had followed the sun in his retreat, sought their old homes, with strange tales of their travels.

But votaries of the changing moon were themselves a fickle and restless folk of varying moods, though when a great discontentment arose again it was through their devotion to steadfastness. It was the old craving for a greater familiarity with the gods, which we find among the most religious races of mankind, that led the people to their new discontent. Only for a part of the time could they worship the inconstant moon, and the priests felt that when its face was turned from them there was a laxity of discipline which could not fail to be serious. So the tutelary Lesser Spirit was again implored to intercede for them and obtain the gracious favor of a more continuous revelation of the presence of the Manitou. They wished to see him and worship him daily and hourly if need be. The Lesser Spirit received their message, but in departing with it for the gate of heaven he bade them farewell forever.

Soon after the great mountain was wrapped in dense clouds with thunders and lightnings. The mountain shook and the hills and plains vibrated as under the heavy blows of earthquake shocks. Day after day passed in terror until at length the clouds cleared away and all was calm again. Then, lo, a great light fell from the open portals of heaven full upon the towering mountain top which was at its threshold. And there from the highest point of the peak shone down upon them a majestic and godlike Face. Far out upon the plains, far as the heaven-meeting peak could be seen, its features were manifest to all, filling the observers with awe and an unknown sense of the power and nearness of the Manitou. As a final seal of sacredness the mark of the symbol which had already of old been stamped upon

the face of the sun and the moon, was now set
upon the earth, and upon the very mountain of
their history and religion. And, the legend is
careful to add, the nation became more unified
and more powerful than ever,

> "Watched over by the solemn-browed
> And awful face of stone."

There seemed now no reason for further
entreaties to the Manitou, whose kind regard

for his chosen had been so signally shown. But with that inspired belief which shows itself in all histories, that religion should stop short of nothing but absolute perfection according to the thinker's own ideas, it was not long before the devout priests felt the need of giving further information to their Overruler. It often happened that while perpetual sunshine and moonlight bathed the plains, dark clouds wrapped the summit of the mountain of the Manitou for days at a time, thus concealing their Keblah, and interrupting their devotions. Sorrow and murmuring rose among the simple people in those days of darkness. They dared not undertake a journey, perform a tribal ceremony, set their traps, plant their maize, or engage in any affair of consequence unless the visible face of the Manitou looked favorably upon them. They were too childlike to worship and 'trust the invisible when the Great Face had once been seen. They would that the veil of clouds which gathered about the summit of the mountains might be dispelled forever.

After suns and moons of hesitancy and of

longing for the counsel of the departed Lesser Spirit, the people were emboldened to send an embassy of priests and princes up the stairway of the mountain to the gate of heaven, with their petition to the Manitou. The last three steps of this vast stairway are still plainly seen just north of Cheyenne Mountain, and bear the modern names of Monte Rosa, Mount Grover, and Mount Cutler. Amid the prayers and sacrifices of the people these departed on their unprecedentedly presumptuous and hazardous mission to the Face of the Manitou, the gateway of heaven, and were never heard of more. Terrible was the punishment of their sacrilege in thus approaching the inapproachable. Violent storms enveloped the mountain to its very base in fire-riven folds of darkness. Great rocks came ruining down its precipitous sides, or fell from the clouds, and night succeeded night with no intervening comfort of light. The people fled in terror from their quaking homes, and scourges of bitter rain and biting hail drove them far out upon the plains. These tremendous convulsions threw them prostrate with fear with their faces in the dust. For dust, as though the mountain were ground to powder, filled the air, and has filled it many and many a time since in the region about the base of the peak, in commemoration of those days of reproof, when the stricken inhabitants of the earth realized that they were but as the dust of it, and were bowed in sack-cloth and ashes. At last when the anger of the Manitou was appeased the clouds of wrath rolled away, and the sun and moon and blue sky came once more. What was the bewilderment and awe of every beholder to see that the top of the sacred mountain had disappeared altogether, and no longer reached more than half way to the gate of heaven. Mortals should never again pass over that lofty stairway. The presumptuous ambassadors of the people had been hurled from the high threshold, and the top of the mountain cast upon them, like Ætna on Enceladus. It is a wonder that no Spanish priest has here woven in some fable of confusion of tongues and dispersion of races, but it comes later in the story.

Though with angry reproof, their prayer

had been answered. For on the plain before them, at the foot of the great peak, rose their colossal Palladium, that very threshold stone of heaven, the topmost step of the stairway of spirits, the summit and crown of the old peak, still bearing upon it the Great Face of the Manitou. Never again were the people presumptuous in their religion; and never again was the Face concealed from them, however heavy the clouds upon the peak, except when the spirits were displeased with the nation.

To this day whoever looks from any point on the site of the old capital of the aborigines, where now stands the City of Colorado Springs, the city of refuge, can still see the calm, benignant features of the old god of these early Aztecs, on the side of Cameron's Cone, the old summit of the discrowned peak. The snows of winter hide its features for weeks at times; and when the noonday sun shines full in its face, the ancient superiority of the day-god is shown, for the features are then an indistinguishable mass of light and shadow. But through Spring, Summer, and Autumn, in the afternoon shade, or in the fullness of the morning light, it towers in the west like a clear vision. More majestic than the Zeus Otricoli, grander in design and proportions than the fabled dream of carven Athos, it stands as the most perfect, the sublimest of the sculptures with which unaided Nature or the skill of man has adorned the earth. One is slow to believe that Nature alone could so closely mimic the majesty of art, but it is impossible that Aztec hands could have wrought out such a colossal conception.

> "'Twas Nature's will who sometimes undertakes
> For the reproof of human vanity
> Art to outstrip in her peculiar walk."

To one who would learn how step by step the savage mind groped onward, "through Nature up to Nature's God," it is clearer than all theological lectures.

For many generations the favored nation increased in strength and intelligence. But at length a barbarian host, apparently from the northeast, came pressing upon them with the sweeping onslaught of a herd of buffaloes, with the fierceness of mountain lions. It may likely have been this very invasion which furnished to the laureate Southey the material for his noblest epic, the story of Madoc and the Aztecas of the Missouri Valley. The religious people of the peak, relying upon their gods alone, fell back before them until their very sanctuary was oppressed and profaned.

It is true that in earlier times, when they were weaker in number and skill at war, such reliance had not been disregarded. For once a host of giants and of monsters had attacked them from the hostile north, before whom all resistance had seemed utterly vain. And then a great wonder had taken place. The Manitou had turned his mountain face, even as the face of an Ægis, upon the invading bands, and straightway each and all had changed to stone! It was a terrible sight indeed for future enemies to behold that gorgonized army of granite giants standing athwart all paths approaching from the north or northeast, no longer besiegers, but unwilling and silent defenders whom no foe had yet found courage to approach. And though flood and tempest have overthrown and buried many of them, yet by Austin Bluffs and still more in the strange, grim forms which give name to the world-famous Monument Park, the routed remnants of that ancient army may still be seen, some standing defiant with shield and club uplifted to meet the crash of Death's petrific mace, some crouching in eternized horror at their impending doom.

But though the present had living witnesses of the truth of this encouraging tradition, yet the children of the Manitou had no longer any right to expect such needless intervention, and finally, encouraged by supernatural signs they turned against their enemies and repulsed them from their shrines.   But on the day after the battle the sun arose eclipsed, clouds veiled the hills, and a great flood rolled southward from the mountain valleys.   When light was restored to them after a long tempest, lo, the air was filled with omens.   As once before beasts and birds were passing southward in the path of the waters, winds were blowing and strange clouds drifting in the same direction. The scouts brought word of a mighty mustering of myriads of the enemy from the north.

In the midnight sky auroral warriors, red with slaughter, danced the war dance and menaced them with destruction. And most terrible, most astounding of all, the Great Face which had hitherto turned lovingly and fully upon them, now looked away to the south! It, too, had been eclipsed and turned in a single day.

There was but one interpretation of the omens. Plainly they were to forsake their old kingdom, which had grown less and less fertile, and less able to support the increasing numbers of later generations. But all that was good should go with them. The changed face of the Manitou intimated that his watchful care would still follow them in their new home, nor would he look with favor upon the usurpers. The flood of water told that tides of fertility awaited them. The departure of birds and beasts in advance of their march showed that Nature was still their faithful steward. Yet they felt with sadness that because they had allowed sacrilegious invaders to violate the great sanctuary, they must henceforth be expelled from the immediate presence of the Manitou.

With the departure of this interesting people from the cradle and home of their history,
the chapter of their story which concerns us
most is led to a natural end.   Indeed it would
be difficult to continue it, for such records of
their wanderings as have been found are vague
and incomplete; no two writers would interpret them alike.   For these people mingled
with others and lost their individual identity
when they entered the broad path to Mexico
over which such extensive migrations were
then passing.   The history of no one of the
Nahuan nations is intelligible for its migratory
period.   Though the progressive line of archi-
tectural ruins stretching across the plains and
down the valleys of New Mexico and Arizona
into the Aztec empire, would seem to show the
finger posts of the great marching route of
these nations, yet so barren are the records of
the so-called Cliff-Dwellers and other early
inhabitants of our southwest territory, that
many historians even doubt the connection
between the architects of Casa Grande and of
the palace of the Montezumas.   To our minds
the proofs which may be gathered from the

preceding pages are sufficiently conclusive for our purpose. And it is not impossible that further researches among the records of these mediæval, these Dark Ages of aboriginal history, may set our conclusions beyond the reach of skepticism. If our little sketch be the means of suggesting to one reader how much there is of pleasure, of poetry, of truth, of religion, in Nature and natural associations,—if it be the means of prompting more thorough investigation and more careful preservation of every scrap of tradition now vanishing among the races of aboriginal America, we shall feel that it has not been written in vain.

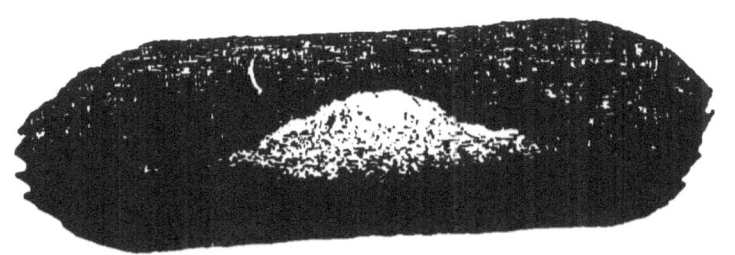

JACKSON'S CELEBRATED PHOTOGRAPHS
OF AMERICAN SCENERY.

COLORADO, PACIFIC COAST, YOSEMITE, YELLOWSTONE PARK, OLD
AND NEW MEXICO.

Size 5x8 inches, unmounted.........................per dozen, $1.50
   5x8   "   mounted.............................   "   2.00
   7x9   "   unmounted.............................each, .50
   7x9 . "   mounted.................................   "   .65
 10x13 "   unmounted.............................   "   .85
 10x13 "   mounted...............................   "   1.00
   5x8   "   colored...............................   "   .75
   7x9   "   "   ....   "   1.50
 10x13 "   "   ....   "   2.50
 22x26 "   "   ....   "   6.00
 22x26 "   plain.................................   "   2.50

Large Panoramic Photographs in sizes from 24x48 inches to 24x80 inches, plain and colored; prices from $7.50 to $36.00, according to size and finish. These Photographs are always in stock, and sent to all parts of the world by

THE CHAIN & HARDY
BOOK, STATIONERY AND
ART CO.

WHOLESALE AND
     RETAIL AGENTS   Catalogues on Application.
FOR COLORADO.

COLORADO WILD FLOWER BOOKS.

These beautiful Books are elegantly and artistically made, and contain pressed flowers of Colorado and the Rocky Mountains. These flowers are perfectly prepared and retain their natural colors. They make a handsome and oppropriate souvenir of this Western country. Sent post paid on receipt of the following prices :

No. 1...each, $0.25
    2..   "   .50
    3..   "   .75
    4..   "   1.00
    5..   "   1.50
    6..   "   3.00
    7..   "   5.00
    8..   "   8.00